D0093636

THE SECRET EXPLORERS
AND THE SMOKING VOLCANO

CONTENTS

Chapter One
AN EXCITING EXPERIMENT

"Almost...done..." said Cheng, leaning over the model volcano he had made. He was gluing pieces of brown and gray paper to the sides so they would look like rock. Outside his kitchen window, the Beijing traffic honked and bicycle bells jangled. Cheng's little sister, Mei, was watching him.

Cheng glued the last bit of paper in place.

"It's finished!" Mei said.

He grinned. "Now for the fun part!"

Cheng filled a plastic bottle with a mixture of baking soda, dish-washing liquid, and water. He lifted up the cardboard volcano and tucked the plastic bottle underneath, so that the open bottle top peeped out of the crater at the top. Then he took some vinegar and mixed it up with some red food coloring in a small cup.

"You can do this part," he told Mei with a smile. "Be careful, though!"

Mei poured the red liquid carefully into the volcano bottle, just the way Cheng showed her.

Right away the contents of the bottle started fizzing and bubbling, filling the little kitchen with hissing sounds.

And then... it erupted!

Red liquid shot up and flooded down the sides of the cardboard volcano. Mei squealed with delight.

"Lava is so cool!" she said.

"I know!" said Cheng, laughing. "It's not real lava, of course. Real lava is molten rock, which comes out of a split in the Earth's crust." For a moment, Cheng imagined a real volcano: the roar of the explosion, the glowing lava, the rotten-egg stink of the sulfur gases. *Maybe one day I'll see a volcano up close*, he thought.

Mei skipped off to do her homework. Cheng began refilling the volcano.

It took a few moments before he realized something was glowing nearby. A circle with a needle in the center, burning as bright as lava on the front door of the house. Cheng read the letters N, S, E and W shining around the edges of the circle, and whooped. It was the compass symbol of the Secret Explorers!

He touched the glowing compass badge on his T-shirt, which matched the symbol on the door, and grinned to himself. The Secret Explorers symbol only appeared when there was a mission. And Cheng was so ready for a mission.

He put his hand against the door and pushed. Right away, the door swung open. Cheng walked into a dazzling white light that made his eyes water. A strong wind rippled over his body, making his T-shirt flap against his skin. For a moment, Cheng felt as if he was flying through the air like a bird.

The light faded away and the wind dropped. Cheng was back inside the Exploration Station!

Glass cases stood around the room,

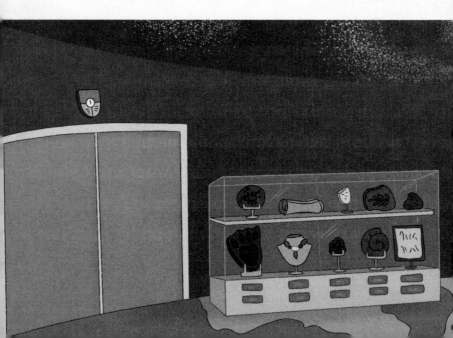

filled with things like the fossil of a dinosaur footprint, an ancient Aztec necklace, a meteorite from outer space, and other objects the Secret Explorers had brought back from their missions. Set into the black stone walls was a bank of computers, ready to monitor the next mission. Comfy chairs and sofas sat grouped together. On the floor was a huge map of the world, and the domed ceiling showed the glittering Milky Way.

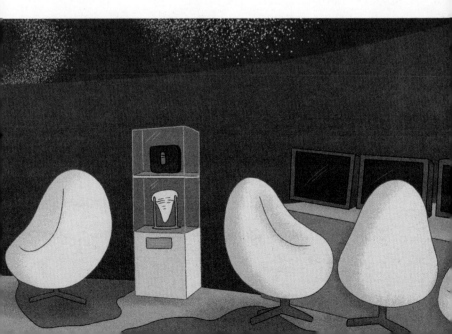

"Cheng—here!" he called.

The air flashed and glowed as the other Explorers began to arrive.

"Tamiko—here!" said a girl with short black hair pinned back with a Stegosaurus hair clip. Tamiko loved dinosaurs.

"Ollie—here!" said a red-haired boy, plonking himself down on the cushions. Ollie knew all about rainforests.

"Roshni—here!" said a girl with long dark hair. Her subject was space.

"Leah—here!" The tall girl saluted as she strode into the room. Leah loved nature and animals.

A girl wearing glasses was next. "Kiki— here!" she said. Kiki was the technology expert of the group.

A boy with a bright smile bounded in next. "Gustavo—here!" he said.

Gustavo's subject was history.

The last Explorer arrived, shaking water from his wading boots. "Connor—here!" he said. He knew everything about life in the oceans.

The Secret Explorers all looked down as a light appeared on the map on the floor, showing the location of their mission. It was coming from a small group of islands in the Pacific Ocean. Cheng felt a surge of excitement.

"Vanuatu!" he exclaimed.

"Bless you," said Ollie.

Cheng chuckled. "Vanuatu, the country. That's the name of those islands," he said. "Vanuatu has a volcano. That's how I know about it."

A little screen appeared in the center of the island group. It showed a cloud of gray ash coming out of a large black mountain.

"That's Mount Yasur," Cheng exclaimed. "Some volcanoes are dormant and don't erupt anymore, but that one's active."

"Doesn't that mean it's really dangerous?" asked Roshni.

Gustavo looked worried. "During Roman times, a volcano called Vesuvius destroyed the city of Pompeii!"

"Don't worry, some active volcanoes only have small eruptions," said Cheng. "Mount Yasur is one of them! You can get up close and look."

Cheng's compass badge lit up—he had been chosen for the mission! He punched the air in delight. He was going to see a real volcano!

Leah looked down at her own glowing badge. "Looks like it's you and me, Cheng," she said. Her eyes shone. "The soil near volcanoes is really fertile, so I bet there are some amazing plants. And amazing plants usually means amazing animals, too."

Kiki pulled down a lever set into the wall. A rickety old go-kart rose out of the floor. It had two flaky red wooden seats and four worn wheels.

"Hey there, Beagle," said Leah with a grin. "Looking as beautiful as ever."

The Beagle was named after Charles Darwin's famous exploration ship. It was the Secret Explorers' mission vehicle, and it held more secrets and surprises than anyone could have guessed.

The other Secret Explorers took their places at the computer terminals, ready to help Leah and Cheng during the mission.

"Good luck," said Gustavo. He looked solemn. Cheng guessed he was still thinking about Vesuvius.

"Don't fall into any craters," advised Connor.

But Cheng wasn't scared—this was all he'd ever wanted!

Cheng and Leah settled themselves in the Beagle. Cheng rested his hands on the broken-looking steering wheel. It felt warm under his fingers.

"Ready?" he asked Leah.

She grinned.

Cheng pressed the Beagle's "START" button. The old vehicle gave a shudder and a jolt, accelerating away. The air filled with a light so bright that Cheng had to lift one hand from the steering wheel to shield his eyes.

The Exploration Station and the other Explorers vanished. Cheng felt excited as the Beagle's old steering wheel changed into a solid joystick beneath his hands.

He blinked. Blades whirled above them. The **WHUPWHUPWHUP** sound they made was muffled by the headset now around his ears.

Chapter Two
EXPLORING THE ISLANDS

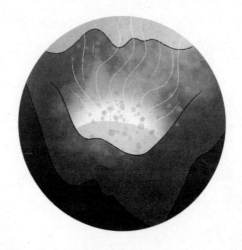

Cheng gazed down into the huge mouth of Mount Yasur. The molten rock in the volcano's crater glowed a fierce orange red. It looked like the skin of a bright, glowing animal that moved and breathed. Every now and then a little spout of glowing lava shot into the air. Clouds of ash rolled above the burning heart of the volcano.

"Wow," gasped Cheng. He turned to Leah, who was sitting beside him. "This is amazing!"

The helicopter was pretty cool too. It had a curved windshield, and lots of levers and controls that made Cheng's head spin. Cheng was glad the Beagle had given them headsets so they could hear each other clearly, because the helicopter was noisy.

Behind the pilot's seat the helicopter's floor was gleaming metal. Stowed away were high-visibility clothing, cables and ropes, and something that looked like a bed.

"A stretcher," said Leah. "This is a rescue helicopter! The winch is outside, look." And she pointed out of the window to the winch attached above the outer door.

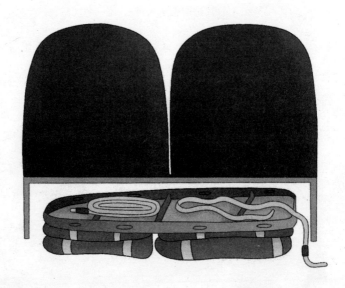

The Beagle made a loud **BEEP**. Lights began to glow on the control panel, showing them how to steer the helicopter.

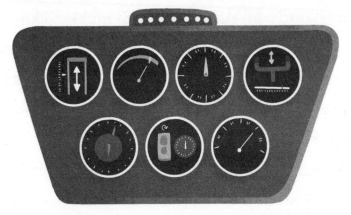

"I think I get it!" Cheng took the controls. "The joystick makes it go forward and backward, this lever makes it go up and down, and these pedals make it spin. Hold on!"

He pushed a pedal with his foot. The Beagle obediently spun around, its blades beating through the air. Cheng used the joystick to level, and the helicopter flew steadily away from the crater.

"Let's fly around," he suggested to Leah. "We need to find out what our mission is."

Cheng gazed out of the windshield at the islands of Vanuatu. They looked like a string of green jewels stretched across the water. The beaches were splashes of white on the edges of the island. The darker green patches were swamps and lowland forests. The bright green of the rainforest stood lush and tall in the interior.

"The islands form a Y-shape," Leah said, squinting down. "Why are they scattered around like that?"

"Volcanoes," explained Cheng. "Over millions of years, volcanoes on the seafloor erupted over and over again. Each eruption built up a new layer of rock. Gradually the volcanoes grew bigger and bigger, until they rose above the ocean to make islands. Isn't that amazing?"

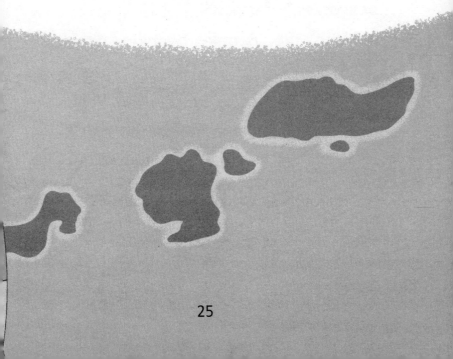

The Beagle *BEEPED* in agreement.

But there was still no sign of their mission.

"We should land somewhere," said Cheng, tearing his eyes away from the view. He flew steadily along the coast, looking for somewhere to come down.

"There!" exclaimed Leah, pointing at a circular landing pad in the middle of a patch of bright-green rainforest with a large H printed in the middle for "helicopter." "Perfect!"

With the Beagle beeping directions, Cheng carefully lowered the helicopter. It was tricky, and he had to concentrate. When the runners beneath the Beagle touched down, Leah cheered. She unhooked herself from her headset, unbuckled her seatbelt, and threw open the door. Cheng scrambled out as well.

They walked together down a path

leading into the trees. The air was heavy and humid, and full of birdsong. There was a gentle **DRIP DRIP DRIP** of leaves around

them, and the wet earth smelled rich and strong.

"What do you think the mission is going to be?" Leah wondered aloud as they followed the path. Heavily scented flowers hung over their heads, and vines crisscrossed the trees above them. "Maybe we're supposed to stop the volcano from erupting. I mean, imagine the damage it would do to all this!" She waved her arms at the beautiful vegetation.

"But stopping an eruption is impossible," said Cheng. "It's too powerful. It must be something else . . ."

Leah suddenly gasped. She grabbed Cheng's arm. "Look up there!"

Cheng squinted up at the trees. Four enormous bats were hanging from an branch overhead. One of the bats unfolded its leathery wings, revealing a pointed furry face. Cheng smelled a waft of something strong and musky as it flapped away. Its wingspan was enormous!

"Flying foxes!" Leah said gleefully. "Most people call them fruit bats. They're native to

Vanuatu. All the other land mammals here were introduced by humans."

"They look like bats from a vampire movie," Cheng said a little weakly.

"Their Latin name is *Pteropus vampyrus*," Leah told him.

Cheng started in shock.

"They aren't actual vampire bats," Leah said, laughing. "They only eat fruit and drink flower nectar."

Cheng felt more than a little relieved.

As they walked, Leah identified the other animals and birds around them. The bright feathers of birds like chestnut-bellied kingfishers and the royal parrot finches glimmered in the branches. Ahead flitted a black butterfly with large blue spots on its wings. "That's called a great egg fly," said Leah. "Or a blue moon butterfly, which I think sounds nicer!"

A scrabble in the undergrowth made Cheng jump. "Scrub fowl," Leah told him, as a large black bird with a red, scaly head hurried across the path. "They bury their eggs in the warm soil near volcanoes to keep them warm until they hatch."

Cheng thought that was pretty cool.

The trees began thinning out as the path led into a clearing.

"It stinks," said Leah, wrinkling her nose.

"That's sulfur," said Cheng. "It's a gas from the volcano."

They emerged from the forest to see groups of people talking and laughing around a wide, steaming blue pool.

"Hot springs!" Cheng exclaimed. He kicked off his shoes and ran to the edge of the pool, dipping his toes into the water.

Leah paddled into the water beside him. "Wow, it's warm! Like a bath or something."

"It's being heated up by the rocks it flows through," Cheng told her. "The rocks are warm because they're being heated by magma from the volcano."

"Mag what?" said Leah.

"Magma is hot molten rock," Cheng explained. "It comes up through the Earth's

crust to make volcanoes. I bet this pool is 140°F"

Cheng watched as a group of local people pulled a tightly sealed bag out of the water, amid talk and laughter from the tourists surrounding them. As the bag was unsealed, a delicious, spicy smell wafted toward Cheng.

"Wow," said Leah. "The water's so hot, those people just cooked their lunch! How cool is that?"

There was a sudden shout. Cheng caught a glimpse of black and tan fur. Several of the people gathered around the cooking jumped backward as a small puppy hurtled past them, splashing merrily through the edge of the pond, drenching them all in hot water. A couple of people tried to grab the puppy, but it was having too much fun and dodged their hands.

"Who does it belong to?" Leah wondered aloud.

"Good question," said Cheng.

No one seemed to be looking around, or calling the puppy's name. The little dog splashed the water, wagging his little tail and dashing in and out of everyone's legs. Cheng felt worried.

He pushed up his sleeves. "We'd better try to catch it," he said. "This terrain is dangerous. If it runs off, who knows what will happen!"

Chapter Three
MAKING FRIENDS

Cheng broke into a run, splashing through the steaming springs, doing his best to keep his eye on the puppy. For such a little thing, it was fast! Cheng sped up. Leah was just behind him.

The trees beyond the hot springs were thinner than the rainforest they had left behind. Cheng caught glimpses of the ocean through the twisting trunks and branches, and found he was closer to the beach than he'd realized. The roar of the surf thundered ahead as he ducked under the overhanging branches, startling a few birds with leaf-green plumage. The birds skittered into the sky with alarm.

Cheng and Leah stopped on the edge of a wide, curving beach.

"Where'd that puppy go?" Leah asked through panted breaths.

The sound of the surf was louder here, with breakers smashing and foaming on the white sand. Cheng glimpsed surfers bobbing around in the waves, riding brightly colored boards. Their glistening black wet suits reminded Cheng of sea lions.

Cheng shaded his eyes. The puppy crouched in the sand several yards in front of him, looking back with wide brown eyes.

"There you are!" he said, and started to run again.

Right away, the puppy sprang to its feet and took off down the beach.

"Come back!" he roared, running faster.

The puppy wasn't listening. It skipped and dodged, and ran around. It was clearly having the time of its life.

"Cheng, this isn't working!" said Leah, as Cheng tried in vain to grab the little animal, and fell onto the soft sand. "Chasing the puppy is just making it more excited. It thinks this is a game."

Cheng wrinkled his nose in thought. "So how are we going to catch it?"

Leah rubbed her chin. "We make it come to us," she said.

A bright yellow ball was lying in a dip in the sand, near the line of the trees. Leah walked over and picked it up.

"Here we go," she said. "Wish me luck!"

She waved the yellow ball at the puppy. "Come and play, puppy," she said. "Look at this pretty yellow ball. Come and get it!"

The puppy stopped running around, and stared at Leah and the ball. It tipped his head to one side. Then it crouched into the sand, with its bottom in the air and its tail waving.

"It looks like it's going to run away again," Cheng warned, propping himself up in the sand with his elbows.

"Patience," said Leah. She waved the ball again. "Come on, puppy! Come and play!"

The puppy leaped to its feet. It let out a little bark of delight and scampered toward Leah, who scooped it up with her free hand.

"Success!" she said triumphantly, giving the ball to the puppy as a reward.

"Well done, Leah!" Cheng got to his feet and clapped. "Impressive animal knowledge," he said. He went to Leah and gave the puppy a little scratch behind its soft brown ears. "Now all we have to do is find your owner, little guy."

As the puppy squirmed in Leah's arms, Cheng studied the people on the beach. There were families gathered around picnic blankets, and a few people with fishing rods. The surfers rode the waves, bobbing around like brightly colored corks, as the Sun glittered on the water.

Cheng suddenly saw a girl in the distance. She looked a few years younger than him and Leah, and she was searching around the lifeguard stand. She talked to different groups of people walking along the beach. Several of the people paused, and started gazing around them in the same sort of way as Cheng.

Cheng nudged Leah. "She could be the person we're looking for!"

The puppy wiggled in Leah's arms as they made their way across the powdery sand toward the girl.

"Excuse me," Leah began.

The girl whirled around and gasped. "Keemo!"

The puppy yipped with delight.

"I think we've found his owner," said Leah with a laugh. She handed the puppy to the girl.

The girl beamed. "Oh, Keemo, where have you been?"

"Cheng and I found him back there, by the hot springs," said Leah. "I'm Leah, by the way."

"My name's Halani," said the girl. "Thank you for finding Keemo. He's very playful. I've been so worried . . . I was studying the surfers, and I didn't notice him run off."

"Are you learning to surf?" asked Cheng.

Halani nodded. "I love watching the surfers, seeing how they do it. Everyone's crazy about surfing in Vanuatu. Some people even surf down the slopes of the volcano."

Cheng remembered the little screen at the Exploration Station, showing them the erupting volcano. They had saved the puppy, but their mission must be related to Mount Yasur. It wasn't over yet.

He pointed to the conical top of the volcano, which rose above the trees at the edge of the beach. "We'd love to see Mount Yasur up close."

"I'll take you there now!" said Halani. She put Keemo down and clipped his leash onto his collar. "Come on, Keemo. You need a walk to tire you out!"

This was it! Cheng was going up a volcano.

Chapter Four
UP THE MOUNTAIN

Halani chattered happily to Leah and Cheng as they made their way from the beach toward a path that wound through the trees toward Mount Yasur. She was clearly delighted by how much Leah knew about the island's wildlife. Keemo rushed ahead, tugging on his leash and wagging his tail.

The path grew steeper, and the trees began to thin out as they reached the slopes of the volcano. Now Cheng saw other people walking up it also. The earth beneath his feet grew darker. Soon, the vegetation died away entirely, and the ground was just rock. The smell of sulfur was growing stronger, and the earth felt warm. Cheng imagined the magma beneath his feet, churning and boiling and bubbling like a great witch's cauldron. It gave him a thrill.

A flash in the sky made Cheng look up. His mouth dropped open. A great fountain of lava shot out of the crater, hissing and glowing.

"Wow," he breathed. He was witnessing a real, live volcanic eruption! It was a dream come true.

At last, they reached the top of the volcano. Around the crater, a lot of visitors were having guided tours, looking around and taking photos.

"They're pretty close to the edge," said Leah. "What if there's a really big eruption?"

"That's where I come in!" said a voice.

They all turned to see a woman in overalls, bending over a silver box.

Keemo jumped up at her eagerly. The woman patted his head. She was tall, with curly hair and glasses. "Hi, little guy! You're friendly, aren't you?"

Cheng was staring at the silver box on the ground by the woman's feet. It stood on three metal legs that were bent in the middle, and had rows of blinking lights.

"That's my equipment," the woman explained. "It contains seismology devices that monitor the volcano's activity."

Cheng's eyes widened. "You're a volcanologist? That's so cool!" Volcanology was the perfect job. Imagine spending all day, every day, studying volcanoes!

The woman nodded. "That's right, I'm a volcanologist! My name's Elenola. I've been working on Mount Yasur for several months now."

Leah studied the box's silvery legs. "It looks like a crazy metal spider," she said.

"That's what we call it!" said Elenola. "A Spider. This Spider picks up information about the volcano, such as changes in the gases around it and any movement within the ground. Then it sends the information to an observatory, where scientists look at it. They use the information to predict when Mount Yasur is going to have a big eruption, so they can evacuate the volcano."

"Evacuate?" said Leah, looking a little alarmed. Keemo yapped happily.

Elenola laughed. "Don't worry. Large eruptions are very rare. It's only when the buttons light up . . ."

Her voice trailed off. The lights had suddenly lit up along one side of the Spider and there was a whirring sound inside the silver box. It sounded like it was picking up speed, like an accelerating car. Cheng saw a flash of panic in Elenola's eyes.

"The volcano's going to erupt," he guessed. "Isn't it?"

The scientist had already taken out her phone. "I'm calling the observatory," she said. "Hello? Yes, this is Elenola, I'm on Mount Yasur . . . Yes, that's what I'm calling about . . . Are you picking up the readings?" She listened for a few moments. "Right," she said at last. "Of course. Understood." She pocketed the phone. "You're right," Elenola said to Cheng. "It looks like an eruption is coming!"

Cheng stared anxiously at the tourists with their cameras and backpacks, enjoying the view of the edge of the volcano. "We need to get everyone out of here," he said.

The local guides were studying their phones and shaking their heads. It looked like they had picked up the warnings about the eruption too. They started gathering the tourists together and leading them to the path back down the volcano.

A spout of lava rose above the lip of the crater. *It's higher than the last time!* thought Cheng. *Amazing!*

He pointed at the swirling clouds emerging from the crater. "That looks like smoke," he said to Leah, "but it's actually water vapor, and sulfur gas, and carbon dioxide—"

"We have to go!" Leah cut him off. "It won't be long before the volcano erupts for real!"

She was right. They had to get off the volcano, and fast!

Chapter Five
ERUPTION!

They followed Elenola off the peak, trekking along the well-worn path which ran down the side of Mount Yasur. Cheng felt the heat of the volcano beneath his feet. It was incredible to think that he was standing directly above trillions of tons of boiling, molten rock.

"Is the Spider going to be OK?" Leah asked.

"Oh yes," Elenola said. "It will stay where we left it and continue monitoring the activity for the observatory. There's a great viewpoint up ahead, where we'll be able to watch the eruption from a safe distance."

Cheng was pleased they wouldn't miss it.

They trekked on, following the path. The sides of the mountain swooped down into the bright green rainforests below, and the ocean sparkled along the sandy beaches.

Elenola pointed to a large group of rocks a short distance ahead of them, where one or two of the tourist groups were already standing and looking back at the crater. "That's where we're going," she said.

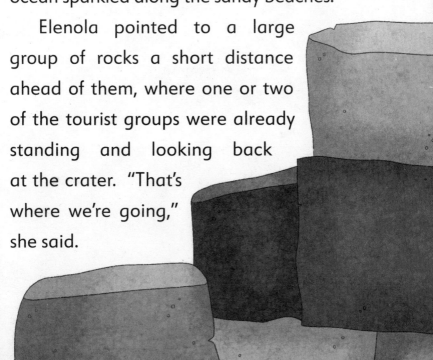

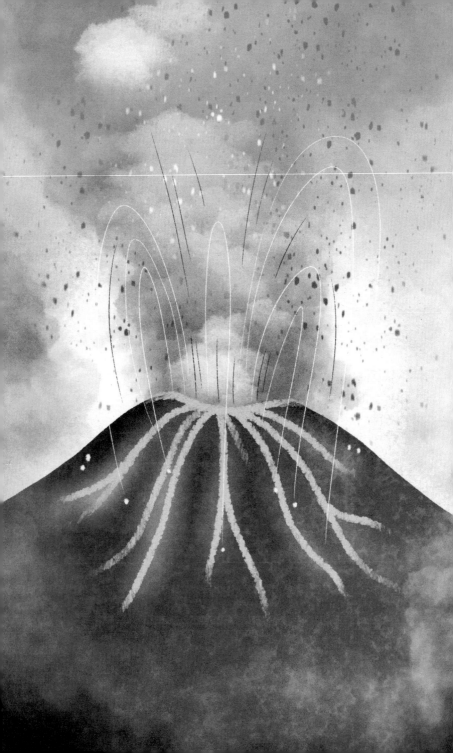

As soon as Cheng and Leah reached the rocks, there was a hollow, booming sound behind them. Red molten rock shot out of the crater, jetting fifteen or twenty yards into the air. The eruption lit up the clouds, creating crazy patterns and shadows in the swirling mass of water vapor and gases.

"This is so cool! But why exactly is it erupting?" Leah asked curiously.

"Well, the Earth is made up of different layers," Cheng said. "It has a superhot center, then a layer of solid rock called the mantle, and then the crust, which is the part we're all standing on. The crust is made up of tectonic plates, which are kind of like gigantic paving stones."

He paused as a huge spray of lava shot out of the crater.

"Whoa! Anyway, some of the tectonic plates are pulling apart, and some of them are pushing together—"

"Wait, the Earth's crust is moving?" asked Leah, her eyes wide.

Cheng nodded. "Don't worry, it's happening really, really slowly. At the edges of the plates, the rocks in the mantle melt to make magma. This magma pushes its way upward—and if it reaches the Earth's surface, a volcano forms! The magma comes out of the volcano, and is then called lava." Cheng pointed at the spouting, grumbling Mount Yasur. "That's what's happening right now!"

They stood watching until the volcano grew quieter, and finally stopped entirely.

"I wonder if Halani's seen an eruption that big before," said Leah. "Where is she, anyway?"

"I haven't seen her or Keemo since we were at the crater," said Cheng.

"Animals can be really sensitive to natural disasters," Leah said, biting her lip. "Maybe Keemo could sense the eruption and ran off."

"Let's ask around," said Cheng. "Maybe someone's seen them."

They started walking around among the groups of tourists, who were beginning to trickle away back down the mountainside. Had they seen a girl with a black and tan puppy?

"Yeah, I saw a dog like that," said a guy with a red backpack. "Back on the crater. It was running away. I think its leash had broken or something."

Cheng and Leah exchanged worried looks. "He was barking a lot, around about the time I was asking Elenola about the equipment," said Cheng.

Leah's face looked pale. "The eruption must have frightened Keemo, and Halani must have gone after him." Her voice cracked. "They're still up on Mount Yasur!"

Cheng's heart was beating hard and fast. He knew what their mission was now. "We're here to save Halani and Keemo!"

"The Beagle!" said Leah. "That's why it's a rescue helicopter this time. We have to fly up to the volcano to save Halani and Keemo, Cheng. As fast as we can!"

They started running down the rocky path which led them back to the rainforest and the beach. The ground skittered and slid under their feet and it was hard to keep their balance, but they kept going. It felt wrong to be running away from the crater if Halani and Keemo were there, but Cheng knew they had no choice. They had to get to the Beagle, and fly it back up the volcano as fast as they could.

The rainforest canopy shaded them as they ran, the vines and leaves hanging above them in the humid air. The sound of the birds was deafening.

Leah paused, resting her hands on her knees. "That's weird," she gasped, trying to catch her breath.

Cheng had to raise his voice over the sound of the birds. "What's weird?"

Leah waved a hand at the treetops. "The birds," she panted.

Cheng squinted up into the treetops. The birds did seem very agitated. Brightly colored feathers swirled overhead as they fluttered restlessly through the trees, chattering and singing as if their lives depended on it.

"They shouldn't be so loud," said Leah. She wiped her face. "This is wrong, Cheng. I think they're sensing that something's up." She looked frightened. "Could these guys know that Mount Yasur is about to erupt again? If that's true, then Halani and Keemo are in real trouble!"

Chapter Six
TIME FOR A RESCUE

The Beagle stood where they had left it, on the landing pad near the hot springs where they had first seen Keemo. Cheng felt a twist of worry in his belly as he thought about Halani and her happy, naughty little puppy.

The helicopter greeted them with a wild flurry of anxious **BEEPS** and flashing lights.

"We missed you too, Beagle," said Leah as she scrambled aboard and slipped on her headset. "You know something's wrong, don't you?"

Cheng leaped into the Beagle after Leah, pulling himself into the cabin and flinging himself down in the pilot's seat. He was too out of breath to do anything but put on his headset and pat the Beagle's controls in greeting. Then he flicked on the communications panel on the dashboard. A screen lit up.

"Calling the Exploration Station," said Leah urgently. She flicked another button. "Exploration Station, do you read us?"

The Exploration Station came into view. The other Secret Explorers had gathered around the screen. Cheng had never been more pleased to see them.

"Are you guys OK?" said Ollie.

"Yeah, how can we help?" asked Roshni.

"We've been tracking you and we know Mount Yasur just erupted," said Gustavo.

"We're worried there's going to be another eruption," Cheng broke in, leaning close to the screen. "And we have a friend with her dog who may be lost up there. Can you intercept the volcanic data being transmitted to the observatory?"

"Just give me a second and I'll be in their database," Kiki said.

It was an anxious wait. Leah and Cheng could hear Kiki's fingers clicking over the computer keys. Cheng looked out of the helicopter windshield, but could only see the banks of trees which surrounded them. From the way Leah kept glancing at the wildly twittering birds among the tangled branches,

Cheng knew she was still worried. He crossed his fingers. Maybe they were wrong about a second eruption.

"Got it," said Kiki. She frowned. "It says there are a lot of gases being released—more than usual. And the temperature of the lava . . . that looks seriously high as well."

Cheng's stomach plummeted. More gases and higher temperatures? That meant Mount Yasur wasn't just going to erupt again. It was going to be a much bigger eruption than before!

"That's bad," he said, when he could find his voice.

"How bad?" asked Leah.

Cheng shook his head. "A lot worse than the last one," he said grimly. "Halani and Keemo are in serious danger."

"Then we need to get up there," said Leah. "But is it possible to fly so close to an eruption?"

"Not in an ordinary helicopter," said Cheng. "The ash would damage the blades. But luckily the Beagle is no ordinary helicopter."

"It definitely isn't," Leah said, patting the

control panel affectionately. "The Beagle will be OK, but I don't think that Spider machine will be . . ."

"The Spider!" Cheng cried. "That's it!" Halani and Keemo were last seen near the Spider. It was a place to start, at least.

"Guys?" he said to the Secret Explorers, who were still standing grave-faced around the screen. "Can you give us a location for the Spider?"

Kiki reeled off the map coordinates. Leah's eyes grew wide as she realized what Cheng was planning. She tapped the numbers into the Beagle's GPS. The screen leaped to life, showing the contours of Mount Yasur. A little dot pulsed on the edge of the yawning crater.

"Got it," said Cheng. "Thanks guys. Over and out!"

"Good luck!" called the other Secret Explorers, before the screen went blank.

The Beagle **FLASHED** and **BEEPED**, guiding Cheng around the control panel. The **WHUPWHUPWHUP** sound of the blades began over their heads, slowly at first and then faster. Cheng increased the throttle. The helicopter rose from the landing pad and lifted clear of the trees.

"We're coming for you, Halani," said Cheng, pushing the joystick forward to steer the Beagle in the direction of the volcano. "Hang in there!"

They circled around to approach Mount Yasur as safely as they could. The air had turned into a fog, thick and gray with ash from the volcano. At first they caught glimpses of the glittering ocean and the green of the rainforest through the swirling ash, but before long they had lost visibility and had to rely completely on Kiki's map coordinates.

Cheng shuddered to think of all the things that could go wrong. They might get the coordinates wrong and fly smack into the side of the volcano! They were truly flying blind.

"See anything?" asked Leah.

Cheng squinted through the thick, smoky air. "No," he admitted. "Maybe if we go a little lower . . ."

A great plume of black ash spewed into the air, surrounding them in darkness.

"I don't like this," said Leah, shivering in the seat beside Cheng.

Cheng didn't like it either. Gritting his teeth, he checked the coordinates again, and flew around what he hoped was the top of the volcano. The Beagle beeped encouragingly, but it was hard to stay positive when they could hardly see the enormous volcano, let alone Halani and Keemo.

The darkness lit up with a brilliant flash as a jet of lava shot up from the volcano. Cheng knew they didn't have long now

before the eruption truly began...

"There!" Leah shouted. She rose in her seat, and tapped the windshield. "Down there, look! I can see them!"

Chapter Seven
CHENG'S BIG IDEA

Through the thick, ashy clouds, Cheng caught a glimpse of something. But the next moment, the clouds hid it from sight again. Cheng groaned. "If only we could see better!"

There was another roar from the volcano and a blast of ash. But then the clouds parted once more. This time Cheng could see that it was definitely Halani! She was sitting down on the gray, rocky side of the volcano. Cheng wondered why. Then he realized that she was holding onto her ankle.

"It looks like she's hurt," said Leah, with a frown of dismay.

Cheng nodded. No wonder Halani hadn't left the volcano when it erupted.

Beside her, more difficult to see through the smoke, was Keemo. The puppy looked as if he was on guard, standing close to Halani with his ears pricked. Cheng guessed he could hear the helicopter.

He looked at the stretcher in the back.

Then he looked at the door, with its external winch.

Cheng knew what he had to do.

"I'm going down there," he said.

"I don't think we can land next to them," said Leah anxiously. "The visibility's too poor."

"I know," Cheng said. He set the controls to automatic, unbuckled himself from the pilot's seat and stood up. "You'll have to winch me down. Take over the controls, Leah. I'm going to rescue Halani and Keemo."

Leah's eyes were wide. "Are you sure?"

Cheng nodded. He was sure.

Leah settled down in the pilot's seat, flicking switches and keeping the helicopter steady. Following the Beagle's helpful beeping and flashing lights, Cheng unbuckled the stretcher from the back of the helicopter. Then he pushed the door open.

The cabin instantly filled with ash, making
his chest tighten.

Keeping his hands as steady as he could,

Cheng attached the stretcher ropes to the winch mechanism. He tried not to look down. When he was confident that all the ropes were attached, he looked across at Leah.

"Pass me a radio," he said, "so we can stay in touch. Can you see how to operate the winch?"

"The Beagle is showing me," said Leah. She pointed at the glowing screen in front of her.

"Thanks, Beagle," said Cheng.

BEEP, BRRRP BEEP, said the Beagle.

"I'll hover, OK?" said Leah. She looked at him and smiled. "You've got this, Cheng."

Cheng nodded. He took a deep breath as he harnessed himself to the stretcher. Then he gave Leah the signal to lower him down.

The stretcher swung and twisted in the

smoky air beneath the
helicopter's belly. Cheng clung
on, keeping his eyes trained on
the ground as it grew closer. It
was scary, but amazing. He
could see the glowing crater
and the sides of the volcano
as it fell away toward the
ocean. Every now and
then, the clouds gave
him a glimpse of the
water.

There   was
another large spout

of lava from the crater. Cheng felt a blast of heat on his skin. The strong smell of the sulfurous gases was making him light-headed.

Halani was below him.

"Halani!" shouted Cheng. He waved, clinging tightly to the lowering stretcher. "Halani, up here!"

Halani looked up. Her eyes widened in surprise and relief. "Cheng!" she said. "Is that really you?"

Keemo started running around in circles with his tail wagging hard. Halani wasn't the only one pleased to see Cheng.

The stretcher touched down. Cheng unharnessed himself and sprang to the ground, hurrying across the rocks to where Halani was sitting. He knelt beside her. "What happened?"

"Keemo was scared by the eruption," Halani said. Her voice was shaky. "He was tugging so hard on his leash that it snapped, and he ran off as fast as he could. I tried to chase him down, but then I fell and twisted my ankle." She rubbed her ankle then looked up at Cheng. "What are you doing here?"

"There's going to be another eruption—a big one," said Cheng. "We have to get you out of here. Can you walk?"

Halani struggled to her feet, holding onto Cheng's arm. She grimaced. She couldn't put any weight on her ankle at all.

The radio clipped to Cheng's belt crackled to life. "Cheng, Cheng, can you read me? Over!"

Cheng lifted the radio to his mouth. "I can hear you, Leah. I've got Halani. I'll get her onto the stretcher and then you can start winching her up. Over."

"We can't. I'm sorry. The ash is so thick up here, I can't see a thing. What if I knock the stretcher against some rocks, or fly into the side of the volcano? It's too risky. I don't know what to do. Over."

The air was growing uncomfortably warm. Sweat poured down Cheng's face, mingling with the dirt and ash. He squinted upward. The winch cable vanished into the clouds above him. He couldn't even see the Beagle anymore. He looked back at the stretcher, and at the sloping, gravelly sides of the volcano.

"I have an idea," he said. "I'm going to release the stretcher from the winch, OK? Then you can wind the cable in. Over."

"Are you crazy?" Leah sounded incredulous. "How are you going to get the stretcher off the mountain? Over."

"Trust me," Cheng replied. "I know how to get us all down. Over." He looked again at the dusty sides of the volcano, the way they swooped into the rainforest below. Then he looked at the stretcher with its solid, flat base, and at Halani's hopeful eyes. Keemo barked, still running around in circles.

"Are you sure? Over."

Cheng could hardly believe he was considering this, but there was no choice. "As sure as I'll ever be," he said. "Over." He ran back to the stretcher, unclipping all the cables so that they dangled in the smoky air.

"The cables are disconnected," he said into the radio. "We'll see you back at the landing pad. Over and out."

The cables rose up into the swirling gas and ash until they disappeared. The volcano grumbled, and another spout of lava spewed into the air. Cheng clipped the radio onto his belt and listened to the **WHUPWHUPWHUP** sound of the Beagle as it faded away into the clouds.

"Has the helicopter gone?" said Halani anxiously. "How are we going to get off the volcano?"

Cheng led her, hopping, toward the stretcher. "Halani, do you remember telling me that some people surf down the volcano?" he asked.

Her eyes widened. "We're going to surf down?"

Cheng nodded. He pulled the stretcher around so it was pointing downhill.

"Cool!" Halani gasped.

Cheng laughed. "Come on, Keemo. You too."

He helped Halani onto the stretcher. Keemo leaped on and snuggled down between Halani's legs. Cheng climbed onto the stretcher behind Halani.

"Hold on tight," he said. He pushed at the gritty soil on either side of the stretcher, moving them forward. The mountainside began to tilt. The stretcher tilted with it. "And here . . . we . . . GO!"

Chapter Eight
A BUMPY RIDE

It felt like they were moving in slow motion as the stretcher bumped and slid over the gravelly path. Cheng pushed again. This time, the stretcher began moving by itself.

"I can't believe we're surfing down Mount Yasur!" said Halani, laughing. She seemed to have forgotten about her ankle in the excitement of the moment, and cuddled Keemo close.

The stretcher was definitely picking up speed, and the warm, sulfurous air on Cheng's face started to feel more like a rushing wind. The stretcher tipped down a steep part of the path.

"Whoa!" shouted Cheng. "WHOA!"

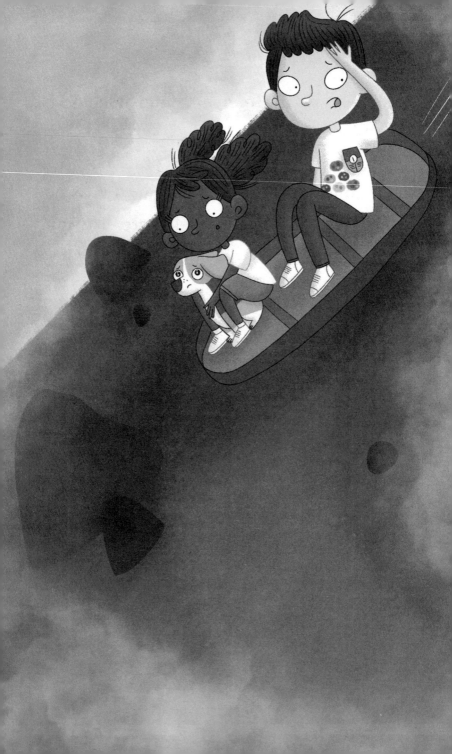

The stretcher was at full speed now, swinging wildly from side to side. They skidded over the rocks, which Cheng knew were a mixture of ash, black solidified lava, and light-gray chunks of pumice—a kind of stone with holes in it like a sponge, which was so light it could float on water. It was formed when rock was thrown out by a volcano. He held his arms out ahead, doing his best to shield them all from flying pebbles and rock fragments.

They were rapidly approaching a curving, right-hand bend in the path. For a dizzying moment, Cheng imagined the stretcher hurtling straight on, and off the edge of the mountain, plunging down into the trees. The ground was racing away from him too fast to put his hands down.

"We need to steer around that bend, Halani!" he shouted through the buffeting air. "Do you have any surfing tips?"

"Yes!" Halani shouted back. "Lean into the curve. Put your weight on the right side of the surfboard—I mean, stretcher. Now!"

Cheng leaned with Halani, putting all his weight into the right-hand side. The metal base of the stretcher groaned and tipped. Cheng could feel the stretcher turning slowly.

They made it around the corner with inches to spare! Cheng leaned quickly to the

left, to avoid oversteering into the mountainside. Halani did the same. Keemo's ears flapped in the wind.

"Teamwork!" Halani yelled, laughing.

"Makes the dream work!" Cheng replied, a little breathlessly.

The path leveled out. Evening was approaching, and the sky on the horizon was beginning to turn a darker shade of blue. The ground began to soften beneath the stretcher, slowing them down. Halani shouted instructions for steering whenever they reached a corner. Cheng concentrated, moving his weight from side to side. Behind them, Mount Yasur shook and rumbled.

Cheng could see the bottom of the path now. Leah was there, waiting with a team of paramedics. They all jumped to the side as the stretcher raced toward them and came, at last, to a bumpy halt.

"How was the ride?" said Leah, grinning.

"Bumpy," Cheng said. He let go of the stretcher and flexed his fingers, which were stiff and sore. "And scary. But it was also pretty AWESOME!" And he

high fived Leah's outstretched hand. Mission accomplished!

Keemo wiggled out of Halani's arms and darted into the undergrowth, his tail wagging. For a moment Cheng wondered if he was going to run off again—but he rushed

back to Halani and licked her cheek as one of the paramedics treated Halani's ankle. It looked like he wanted to keep an eye on his injured owner.

"How is she?" Cheng asked the paramedic.

"It's just a sprain," said the paramedic. "She needs to rest it for a while, and then she should be back to normal."

"Can I go surfing tomorrow?" Halani asked, examining her bandaged ankle.

The paramedic laughed. "Maybe in a

few days! Don't worry, you'll be back on your surfboard soon."

Elenola pushed her way through the group of paramedics. She smiled with relief when she saw Leah, Cheng, and Halani. "I've been very worried about you all," she said. "But it looks as if you made it back down in one piece. And not a moment too soon. The eruption is due at any moment. Get ready, guys. It's going to look spectacular against the night sky!"

A **BOOM** ripped through the air. Cheng twisted around. His mouth fell open as the sky above the crater lit up like a crazy fireworks display. Lava fountained into the air,

golden and glowing, shooting up tons of rock and ash in spectacular formations, glittering like melted gold, exploding from the heart of the Earth. All his life Cheng had wanted to witness something like this. It was everything he'd imagined and more.

They watched until the lava began to quiet down and the rumbling growled and stuttered to a stop.

"Wow," Leah said at last. She looked at Cheng. "No wonder you're crazy about these things."

Cheng couldn't speak, so he nodded instead, and smiled until his face felt like it was going to crack.

"It's been great meeting you," said Leah, hugging Halani. "Enjoy the waves. And Keemo? Be good!"

Keemo barked, as if he understood.

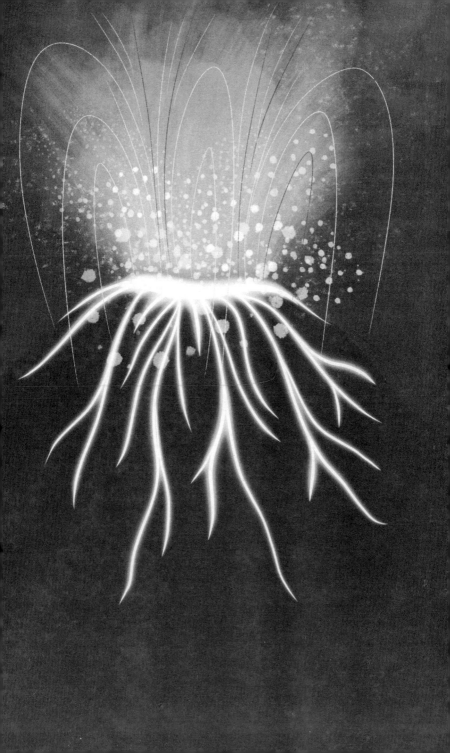

"Thanks for everything," Cheng said to Elenola. "It's been incredible."

Elenola shook his hand. "Good luck with your plans to become a volcanologist. I think you'll be great."

Leah and Cheng waved and moved away, back down the darkening path toward the beach and through the rainforest to the Beagle.

"That was quite an adventure," said Leah, putting on her headset and strapping herself into her seat.

Cheng thought about the beautiful eruption, and his incredible ride down the mountain on the stretcher. "The best," he answered with a grin.

He turned on the Beagle's engine, and they listened to the blades gathering speed over their heads. Then Cheng pressed the "HOME" button on the control panel.

The Beagle rose from the ground at a terrific speed. There was a burst of light. Cheng and Leah were flattened to their seats as the helicopter transformed around them in a blaze of light and wind. Moments later, Cheng felt the headset vanish from his head, and the padded helicopter seat transform back to something hard and wooden. There was a jolt and the light faded.

He opened his eyes.

"Welcome back!" said Ollie, his freckled face grinning.

The rest of the Secret Explorers gathered around the Beagle, congratulating Leah and Cheng on the success of their mission.

Leah stroked the Beagle's splintered old steering wheel. "It's good to be back," she answered Ollie, hopping out of the go-kart.

Roshni's eyes were bright. "Did you bring something back for the Exploration Station collection?"

Cheng began to shake his head—but then he felt something in the pocket of his jeans. He pulled out a piece of rough, light-gray stone.

"Pumice!" he exclaimed. "Volcanic rock. It must have ended up in my pocket when we were

surfing down the volcano."

"When we were surfing down the volcano," Connor quoted back at Cheng, clapping him on the back. "I bet you never thought you'd be saying those words!"

"Pumice?" said Roshni. She took the stone from Cheng and weighed it in her palm. "It's so light! Did you know you can also find pumice on the surface of the Moon?"

"Cool!" said Cheng. He took the pumice

to one of the display cabinets and carefully placed it inside.

"Time to go home," said Gustavo. He pointed to the glowing door set into one of the black stone walls.

Cheng bumped fists with Leah. "Thanks, teammate," he said.

"We had an EXPLOSIVE time!" said Leah with a laugh.

After saying goodbye to the other Secret Explorers, Cheng stepped through the shining door. The wind rushing through his hair reminded him of the way the wind had rushed past on their crazy stretcher ride down the volcano, and the bright light made him think of golden lava.

His hand touched the familiar surface of his own front door. He pushed, and found himself back in his kitchen. Had he really just been watching a live volcano erupting? It seemed impossible. But that was the best part about the Secret Explorers—everything happened for real. He couldn't wait for the next mission.

Mei scampered into the kitchen. "Can we do the volcano again?" she asked. "Can we? And can we make it even BIGGER this time?"

Cheng grinned at his sister. "Sure we can. We can make it the BIGGEST explosion you've ever seen. Now, where's that vinegar . . . ?"

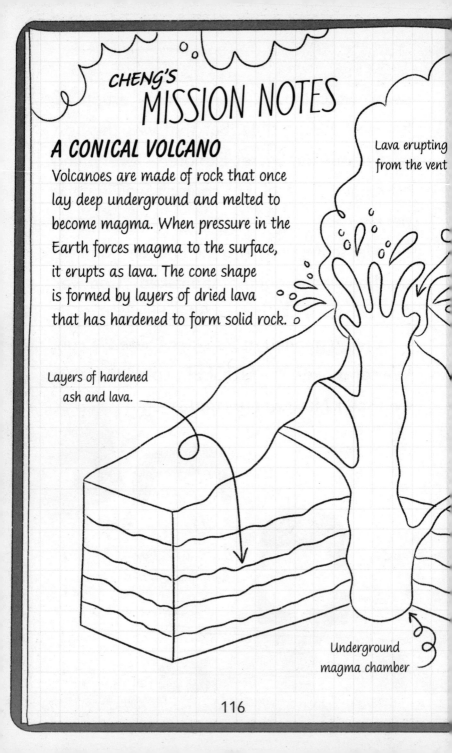

A CONICAL VOLCANO

Volcanoes are made of rock that once
lay deep underground and melted to
become magma. When pressure in the
Earth forces magma to the surface,
it erupts as lava. The cone shape
is formed by layers of dried lava
that has hardened to form solid rock.

Lava erupting
from the vent

Layers of hardened
ash and lava.

Underground
magma chamber

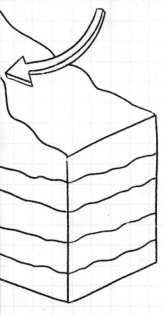

Cloud of ash
and gas

Side vent

LIFE OF A VOLCANO

There are thousands of volcanoes around the world. They are either active, dormant, or extinct.

Active volcanoes can erupt at any time, and their magma chambers are full.

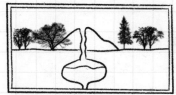

Dormant volcanoes haven't erupted for a while, but they might become active again.

Extinct volcanoes are long dead, and won't erupt again. They have empty magma chambers.

TECTONIC PLATES

WHAT ARE PLATES?

Tectonic plates are like huge jigsaw pieces that make up the Earth's crust. They move very slowly, and when they meet they can cause volcanic eruptions and earthquakes. The biggest ones are shown on this map.

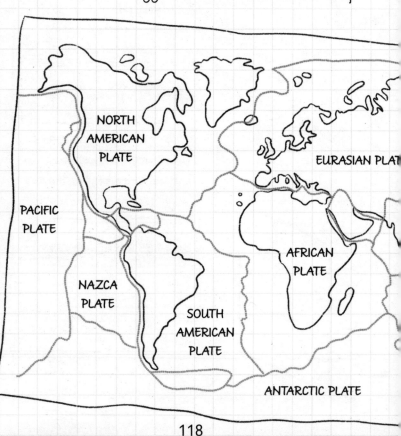

NORTH
AMERICAN
PLATE

EURASIAN PLAT

PACIFIC
PLATE

AFRICAN
PLATE

NAZCA
PLATE

SOUTH
AMERICAN
PLATE

ANTARCTIC PLATE

PLATE BOUNDARIES

The areas where two tectonic plates meet are called plate boundaries. There are three main types of plate boundaries: divergent, transform, and convergent.

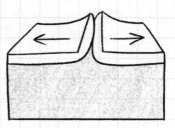

DIVERGENT BOUNDARY
At divergent boundaries, plates move apart, pushed by hot rock from below.

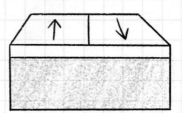

TRANSFORM BOUNDARY
At transform boundaries, two plates scrape past each other.

CONVERGENT BOUNDARY
At convergent boundaries, plates crash into each other, causing one to move under the other.

PACIFIC PLATE

AUSTRALIAN PLATE

MAKE YOUR OWN
ERUPTING VOLCANO

YOU WILL NEED

* Warm water
* Empty plastic bottle
* Baking soda
* Red food coloring
* Dish-washing liquid
* Tray
* Damp sand
* Vinegar

BAKING
SODA

DISH-WASHING
LIQUID

FOOD
COLORING

(1)

Pour warm water into a
bottle until it is almost full.
Add 2 tbsp of baking soda,
then put the cap on the
bottle and shake to dissolve.

(2)

Add a few drops of red food
coloring and a squeeze of
dish-washing liquid. Put
the bottle on a tray.

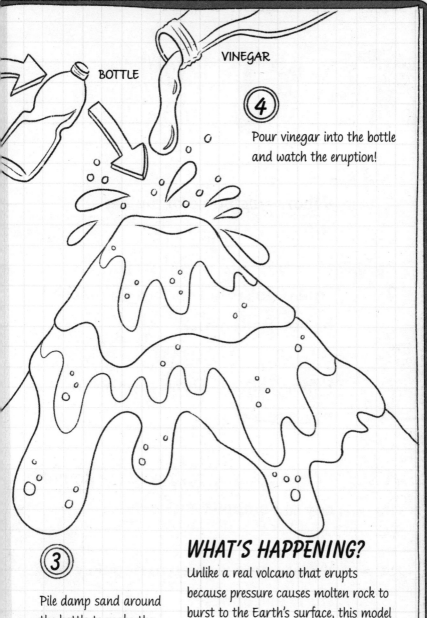

BOTTLE

VINEGAR

4

Pour vinegar into the bottle and watch the eruption!

3

Pile damp sand around the bottle to make the shape of a volcano.

WHAT'S HAPPENING?

Unlike a real volcano that erupts because pressure causes molten rock to burst to the Earth's surface, this model erupts because of a chemical reaction between the vinegar and baking soda.

QUIZ

1   What is the name of the big volcano on Vanuatu?

2   True or false: hot springs are heated by hot molten rock.

3   What other name is given to flying foxes?

4   Which volcano destroyed the Roman city of Pompeii?

5   What name is given to people who study volcanoes?

6   What is the name of the plates that make up Earth's crust?

7   True or false: Volcanologists use a special device called a beetle.

8   Which volcanic rock has holes in it?

SEARCH FOR BIRDS!

There are seven Vanuatan birds to spot in this book. Can you find them all?

They look like this!

Check your answers on page 127

GLOSSARY

ASH
Tiny bits of rock material that have been blown into the air by an erupting volcano

CRATER
A bowl-shaped hole in the top part of a volcano

CRUST
The outer layer of the Earth, where the land is

DORMANT
The word used to describe a volcano that has not erupted in a long time

ERUPTION
When lava, ash, or rock shoots or flows out of a volcano

EVACUATE
When people are moved from danger to a safer place

FERTILE
Land where the soil is good for growing crops

GPS
A system that helps people determine exact locations on Earth and get directions

HOT SPRINGS
Places by volcanoes where hot water from underground bubbles up to the Earth's surface

LAVA
Hot, melted rock that has erupted at the Earth's surface

MAGMA
Hot, melted rock below the Earth's surface

MOLTEN
Metal or rock that has become so hot it has turned to liquid

OBSERVATORY
A place containing scientific equipment used to study nature

PLUME
A long cloud of smoke that looks like a feather

PUMICE
A light volcanic rock that is full of holes

SEISMOLOGY
The study of earthquakes and their effects

TECTONIC PLATES
Giant rocky plates that make up the Earth's crust

VOLCANO
An opening in the Earth's crust, usually in the shape of a mountain, which sometimes erupts

VOLCANOLOGIST
Someone who studies volcanoes

WINCH
A device used to lift heavy objects

Quiz answers

1. Mount Yasur

2. True

3. Fruit bats

4. Vesuvius

5. Volcanologist

6. Tectonic plates

7. False—it's called a spider

8. Pumice

For Zac and Oscar

Text for DK by Working Partners Ltd
9 Kingsway, London WC2B 6XF
With special thanks to Lucy Courtenay

Design by Collaborate Ltd
Illustrator Ellie O'Shea
Consultant Anita Ganeri

Acquisitions Editor James Mitchem
US Editor Jane Perlmutter
US Senior Editor Shannon Beatty
Designer Sonny Flynn
Senior Production Editor Robert Dunn
Senior Producer Ena Matagic
Publishing Director Sarah Larter

First American Edition, 2021
Published in the United States by DK Publishing
1450 Broadway, Suite 801, New York, New York 10018

A catalog record for this book is available from the
Library of Congress.

ISBN: 978-1-4654-9988-2 (Paperback)
ISBN: 978-0-7440-2771-6 (Hardcover)

Printed and bound in Great Britain by
Clays Ltd, Elcograf S.p.A.

For the curious
www.dk.com

The publisher would like to thank: Sam Priddy and Jo Clark;
Sally Beets for editorial assistance; Caroline Twomey for proofreading.